STRANGE SCOUT TALES!

BOOK ONE: HOW TO MERIT IN MONSTERS

MATTHEW CODY

ART BY STEVE LAMBE

RODALE
KiDS

An imprint of Rodale Books
733 Third Avenue
New York, NY 10017
Visit us online at RodaleKids.com.

Rodale Kids books may be purchased for business or promotional use or for special
sales. For information, please e-mail RodaleKids@Rodale.com.

Printed in the United States of America
Book design by Tom Daly

Library of Congress Cataloging-in-Publication Data is on file with the publisher
ISBN 978–1–63565–059–4 hardcover

Distributed to the trade by Macmillan
2 4 6 8 10 9 7 5 3 1 hardcover

CONTENTS

Stand on Your Own Two Feet

 o you like stories about monsters? Secret societies? How about stories about real monsters and real secret societies? Now, I know what you're thinking: there's no such thing as monsters and people who believe in secret societies wear tinfoil hats to keep the "alien thought-probes out."

Well, I don't know about the thought probes, but I can promise you that this story here is totally true. Like, nonfiction-level true—monsters and secret societies and all.

It's also a story about the scouts, and the outdoors, and the three kids who would end up becoming my best friends ever. But I thought leading with the monsters would be more, I dunno, attention-grabby.

My name is Ben Billingsley, and my story begins the day my mom and dad sent me off to the Nature Scouts' sleepaway camp. Maybe you've heard of the Nature Scouts? Maybe you've seen pictures of smiling kids doing all

kinds of outdoorsy stuff like camping, canoeing, and hiking? Maybe those pictures made you want to be a Nature Scout?

Yeah, not me.

See, before that, I was more of what you'd call an indoor kid. Indoor soccer, indoor TV, indoor movies and games.

To me, the outdoors was just the place you had to go through to get back to the inside. No need to hang around in it!

My mom and dad, on the other hand, were always going on and on about camping trips they took when they were younger and bragging about how they once backpacked the

Appalachian Trail before I was born. I don't know what the Appalachian Trail is exactly, but if it's an outdoor thing, I'm glad they already got it out of their systems.

These days their lives are pretty busy with work, so there's no time for camping. That's why, one sticky summer day, I found myself waiting in line with a bunch of other kids outside the entrance to Camp Nature at the base of Bear Mountain. It was my first day as a Nature Scout and my first-ever sleepaway camp. The wooden sign above the gate was simple enough, with the words Camp Nature painted across it in faded letters.

A thick-necked troop leader walked up and down the line reading names off a clipboard. "Collins? Martinez?" When your name was called, you were sorted into one of four troops. I didn't know if the sorting was random or if it was based on the answers we gave to that huge questionnaire they sent home in the mail. If that was the case, then I was in for it.

"Billingsley? Ben Billingsley!"

"Oh, that's me. I'm Ben Billingsley." I'd been too busy weighing my escape plans to hear my own name.

"Pay attention, son! This here's your uniform and *Nature Scouts Handbook,* revised edition. Keep this handbook with you wherever you go, unless you want to be cleaning the latrines!"

He turned to face the rest of the scouts and said, "My name's Bill Spitzer, and I am your Senior Scoutmaster for this year's camp. I don't want to ruin the surprises, but believe me you are in for a camp experience like no other!"

Spitzer gave himself an enthusiastic round of applause.

Maybe two or three kids clapped out of pity. "Now, scouts, you'll find your troop letter posted outside your cabins. Grab a bunk, get changed, and report back here in half an hour."

I raised my hand. "Uh, excuse me. I never got my troop letter."

Spitzer checked his clipboard. "Billingsley, right?" He paused. "Troop . . . D."

Was it my imagination or did someone snicker when Spitzer said my troop letter?

The kid next to me, who looked like he was already shaving, jabbed me in the ribs. "Heh. Troop D! Good luck, dweeb!"

So no. Not my imagination.

Getting Off On The Wrong Foot

Camp Nature was basically a ring of cabins arranged around a wide-open lawn. Beyond that, woods stretched on for as far as I could see. The first few cabins didn't look so bad. They kind of reminded me of those fakey theme-park cabins my family sometimes stayed in when we went on

vacation. You know, where the idea of "roughing it" means the coffee maker only makes one cup at a time. Shiny new vending machines were scattered all around the camp, filled with soda and junk food. Maybe this whole camp thing wouldn't be that bad . . .

"Keep walking, Billingsley!" called

Spitzer. "Those cabins belong to the troop leaders."

More kids started to laugh. This day was starting out swell.

Unfortunately, the scouts' cabins were more . . . cabiny. Each troop had its own pair of side-by-side girls' and boys' basic log cabins. At least they looked clean and sturdy. I saw signs for Troops A, B, and C . . .

But then something barreled into me and knocked me on my butt. I looked up to see the big kid with the five o'clock shadow staring down at me. "Keep moving, dweeb! You gotta long way to go."

He was with a group of what looked like biker-movie rejects disguised as kids.

"Nice, Butch. Score one for Troop C!" said one of them, chuckling.

Of course the kid's name was Butch. Why did bullies always come with tough-sounding bully names? Just once I'd like to get picked on by an Englebert or a Maurice.

So far, I'd seen cabins for Troops A and B and, of course, Troop C. So where was Troop D's cabin?

I ended up trekking all the way to the edge of Camp Nature to find out. There, in the shadows of the mountain forest, were two of the most run-down piles of boards and nails that ever passed for cabins.

"No, it can't be," I groaned.

But it was. On a signpost I found the name I'd been searching the whole camp for: Troop D. Only someone had added a few more letters to the D so that it read: D-W-E-E-B.

Troop Dweeb.

What had my parents gotten me into?

ONE STEP AT A TIME

It took me a few minutes to work up the courage to knock on one of the doors. When I finally did, it seemed to open all by itself.

"What?" someone said.

That's when I realized that the person who'd answered the door was right in front of me, just . . . lower.

A tiny girl in a Nature Scouts

uniform stood in the doorway impatiently tapping her foot.

"Uh, is this Troop D?"

"Can't you read?" asked the girl.

Okay, there was no reason to be rude. "Yeah, but someone's been messing around with the sign."

"Again? Oh, for Pete's sake!"

With an annoyed mutter, she disappeared back inside the cabin and came back a few seconds later with a stepladder, scrub brush, and bucket. Then she marched over to the defaced sign and began viciously scrubbing. "When I find out who did this, I'll make you eat this brush!" she called out to the empty woods.

I didn't think it was possible, but the inside of the cabin looked

even worse than the outside did. The floorboards were loose and squeaked when you stepped on them, and the rafters overhead were like a spider-web city.

There were only two bunk beds, one on either side of the cabin, and neither one looked very comfortable. I'd hardly taken a step inside before someone said, "Hey, wrong cabin!"

It was another girl. Man, was Troop

D nothing but shouty girls? Was this some kind of a joke?

"This is the girls' cabin," she said. "The boys' cabin is next door. And could you please not step on our floor with your shoes on? Sorry, I kind of have a thing about dirt."

"She's a total germophobe!" called the tiny girl scrubbing the sign outside. "Also a hypochondriac."

The other girl rolled her eyes. "I've just had a series of rare and undetectable diseases, that's all. Ginger makes a big deal about everything."

"Uh, no problem. I'll just head over to the boys' cabin."

"Thanks!" She followed me next door. "I'm Asma, by the way."

"Ben."

She had tried to be sneaky about it, but on our way out, I'd caught Asma wiping down the doorknob I'd touched. Oh, brother.

"So, uh . . . am I the only boy?"

"Oh, no." She knocked on the other door. "Manuel? . . . Manuel?"

Ginger poked her head out from the girls' cabin. "He'll never hear you if you don't shout. *Manuel!*"

A boy wearing headphones answered the door. He was deep into his handheld video game. "Oh, hey, bro," he said, without looking up. "Grab a bunk. Can't talk now, no save point, and I've got 2,000 xp to go!"

And just like that, he disappeared back inside.

Asma shrugged. "He's into games."
"Who isn't?"

"No, like really into them. He'll forget to wear shoes if we don't remind him to wear them." As we stepped into the boys' cabin (which was no better than the girls'), she began fogging it up with a can of spray disinfectant. "Some people can be so quirky, right?"

Holding my shirt over my nose and mouth, I tossed my bags onto an empty bunk. "Is this everyone? Just the four of us?"

Asma nodded. "Me, Ginger, Manuel. And now you. We're Troop—"

But we were interrupted by the clatter of something getting smacked. Hard. And again.

K-Clang! K-Clang!

"Gah! Stupid thing!" We rushed outside to see Ginger drop-kicking the bucket. Then she spiked the brush and stomped off.

So, a germophobe, a superobsessed gamer, and a girl with serious anger issues. To tell you the truth, I wondered how I would ever make friends with these kids, or if I even wanted to. But we were stuck with each other.

Welcome to Troop Dweeb.

4

WALK A MILE IN MY SHOES

I've already explained that up until that point I'd never been a big fan of nature. Walking in it, climbing in it . . . stepping in it. So I'd been hoping that they'd keep the first day kind of chill. You know, indoors—someplace with couches, and maybe a

few foosball tables. But no such luck.
Troops A through D gathered on the
assembly lawn in the middle of camp.
Despite my disappointment, the rest of
the kids seemed pretty excited.

Well, not all of them.

"I'm worried that today's going to
be a real workout," Asma was saying.
"I keep two inhalers on me at all times
just for situations like these."

"Oh, what do you need the inhalers for?"

"Well, nothing. Not yet. But you can never be too careful."

Actually, you could. But I kept that comment to myself.

"My mom made me join the scouts so I can move around," said Asma. "I don't get much exercise otherwise."

"Don't you have gym class at your school?"

Asma took a thick, stapled packet of papers out of her pocket. "Doctor's notes. I'm on a strictly limited activity routine due to my poor health."

"Uh, you look pretty healthy to me."

"Yeah, well, Amazonian Brain Fever can appear asymptomatic to people who don't suffer from it."

I stopped in my tracks. "Wait, you have brain fever?"

"Well, no. Not yet." Asma stuffed her doctor's notes and inhalers back into her pockets.

Spitzer was waiting for us on the main lawn. "Okay, scouts! Today you'll meet your troop leader who'll then lead afternoon activities. Tonight's the opening night campfire, and tomorrow we start bright and early with swim lessons at the swimming hole. And thanks to a new corporate sponsorship deal, I've managed to add a few surprises to the swimming hole. No spoilers, but it's going to be great!"

Then Spitzer began calling out the troops by letter to meet their troop leaders for the week. Troop A got a

spunky junior leader named Marcie.
Troop B's leader was mom to two of
the girls, and when you blurred your
eyes you couldn't tell the three of them
apart. And Troop C's bruisers were
assigned to Spitzer (no surprise there).

Every troop got a leader, but what
about us?

Our answer was a loud snore.
It came from a little old man in a
wrinkled troop leader uniform who
was napping in a nearby lawn chair,
his whiskered chin resting on his chest.

"Walter!" said Spitzer. "Walter,
wake up!"

The old man gave a start, knocking
his thick black glasses off his nose.
"Huh? Wassit . . . who in tarnation
went and stole my glasses?"

"They're in your lap, Walter,"
sighed Spitzer. "Troop D, meet your
senior troop leader, Walter Simmons."

The old troop leader grabbed his
walking stick and hauled himself out
of his seat. "I'm awake! I was just
conserving my strength for the big
first day. Eh, where's my troop?"

"Right in front of you," answered Spitzer. "Troop . . . D."

I heard the troglodytes from Troop C snickering at us.

"Hmm." Walter adjusted his huge glasses. He didn't look impressed, but then again I wasn't exactly blown away, either. This guy was old enough to be my great-grandad's great-grandad.

"Okay, Troop D," said Walter. "The rest of you troops, listen up, too. We are Nature Scouts! That means starting with the basics of real scouting. Turn your *Nature Scouts Handbooks* to page 29."

Spitzer cut in. "Eh, Walter, I think as this year's Troop Scoutmaster I should . . ."

But the old man either couldn't hear Spitzer or was pretending he couldn't hear him. "Now you'll find instructions in your books for making the sheepshank knot. Darn useful for a lotta things."

I reached into my back pocket for my handbook . . . and it wasn't there! Oh no, I must've left it back in the cabin, or worse, maybe I'd lost it entirely.

Spitzer's words drifted back to me: "Keep this with you wherever you go, unless you want to be cleaning the latrines!"

My first day at scout camp wasn't even half over, and I was already about to scrub my first toilet.

TROUBLE
AFOOT

faked a bathroom emergency and ran back to the cabins. I hoped my handbook was back on my bunk, but I had a sinking feeling that I'd dropped it earlier that morning when Butch had knocked me on my rear.

The first place I checked was outside Troop C's cabin. I scoured the area but found no handbook. What I found instead was a shocker—a busted-open vending machine and a totally ransacked cabin. The door hung open and it looked like someone had tossed out all of Troop C's pillows and sleeping bags. Was someone playing some kind of camp prank?

Then, in a patch of soft dirt, I spotted a single footprint. A big one. Super extra-large. Man, what did they feed those Troop C kids anyway?

I was measuring that crazy
footprint against my own shoe when
I heard a rustle in the woods behind
me. Actually, it was more than a rustle.
Someone big was moving around in
there, and I could only imagine what
would happen if one of those Troop
C ogres found me snooping around
outside their cabin.

How many kids die every year
from wedgies and toilet-bowl swirlies?

I wasn't sure that those classic camp terrors could actually be fatal, but I wasn't ready to find out, either. So I hid in the bushes and didn't make a sound while whoever it was crashed through the trees behind me. For a moment, he paused and started sniffing the air like some wild animal, but then, thankfully, he continued plodding deeper into the woods.

I didn't need to change my underwear just yet, but I have to admit I was darn close.

Quickly, I made my way to Boys Cabin D and searched all over for my missing handbook. No luck. I double-checked my bedroll and backpack, but the handbook was nowhere to be found. I plopped down on the floor and tried to prepare myself for the horror that was surely the Camp Nature latrines.

That's when I caught a glimpse of something between the loose floorboards. There was a book inside the gap in the floor where the warped boards parted. Maybe my handbook had fallen down there?

It was a tight squeeze, but my arm was just scrawny enough to fit through the gap. (Let's hear it for not exercising!) Unfortunately, I saw right away that this was not my handbook. For one thing, it was all mildewy and gross. And for another, it looked to be about a hundred years old.

Still, when I cleaned off as much of the dust as possible, I could just make out the words "Scouts" and "Book" across the cover. I cracked it open and nearly choked on the dust, but a quick scan of the table of contents showed me the words I needed: sheepshank knot.

Score! This handbook was old and it smelled like a gym sock, but it would have to do. My bathroom emergency excuse would only hold water for so long (no pun intended), and I needed to get back.

I had a knot to tie.

TOE THE LINE

y the time I got back, most of the other troops had finished their knots, even if they were pretty shabby looking.

But Troop D was a disaster. Manuel had somehow managed to tie his hand to his belt loop, and Ginger and Asma were busy trying to get him free.

"Hey, took you long enough in the bathroom," sneered Butch.

Walter cast a sidelong glance at him. "Scouts don't earn badges in sassy talk, son!"

But Spitzer waved him away. "You worry about your scouts, Walter, and I'll worry about mine." He chuckled as he watched Manuel try to get himself untied from his own pants. "Looks like you've got plenty to worry about, too!"

"Troop Dweeb!" someone shouted.

Walter's cheeks glowed red. "Tarnation! Just slow down and follow the directions."

"Here, Butch," said Spitzer, as he handed him a wad of dollars. "Why don't you go fetch your troop mates a round of sodas. We might be here a while!"

There was even more laughter, but I tried to push it out of my mind.

I cracked open my own handbook, brushed away the dust, and found what I was looking for: Knots every scout should know.

It read, "The sheepshank knot is primarily used to shorten a length of rope. But it can also be useful in restraining a chupacabra to avoid nasty bites. For example, the sheepshank can be combined with a goat steak lure to capture this carnivorous critter. See illustration 26."

Wait. A chupa-what?

I turned the page.

What the heck was this handbook talking about? Using a sheepshank knot to tie up some kind of monster! This book was useless. I'd be scrubbing toilets by dinner!

But then I looked a little closer. There were instructions there for the actual knot—you just had to look past all the weird mumbo jumbo about chupacabras and goat steaks. Also, someone had annotated the page with handwritten notes about how much to feed chupacabras, what to give them for treats (um, blood!), and other strange tips.

I couldn't afford to get distracted. Picking up my length of rope, I followed the sheepshank instructions as best I could . . .

And ended up with a perfect sheepshank knot. Unfortunately, because I'd followed the directions precisely, I'd also ended up with a chupacabra snare, but still—the knot part worked!

"Finished!" I cried.

I noticed Walter's eyes drift down to my moldy little handbook, and I quickly stuffed it into my pocket. The old troop leader raised an eyebrow at me, but stayed quiet.

"Lemme see that knot," said Spitzer. He examined the snare. "What's this loopy bit here?"

"Uh, just a little decoration," I lied.

"Hmmphf," snorted Spitzer. "Bit of a show-off, are you, Billingsley?"

"That's not all he is!" We turned around to see Butch stomping onto the lawn. He was red-faced and pointing a meaty finger at me. "That kid wrecked our cabin!"

Uh-oh.

"What's this all about?" asked Spitzer.

"Someone tossed all our stuff out into the dirt and smashed the vending machine!" cried Butch.

"The vending machine!" cried Spitzer. "Those things cost money!"

"I didn't do it," I protested. "It wasn't me!"

Butch smirked. "Then who else? We were all here tying those stupid knots. You're the only one who coulda done it!"

"I didn't do it," I said. "I swear!"

Walter cleared his throat. "Ahem."

Spitzer glanced at him. "You have something to say, Walter?"

"Yep, I do. Seems like there's a lot of accusations flying here but no proof. Butch, did you actually see Ben doing those things?"

"Well, of course not, but who else . . ."

"Raccoons," said Walter. "Those critters get up to all sorts of nonsense."

"Raccoons?" asked Spitzer, dubiously. "Really, Walter, I don't think raccoons could smash a vending machine."

"But a skinny ten-year-old kid

could? Phooey." The old troop leader hiked up his britches. "With no better evidence, I'm going with the raccoons. In the meantime, we can all help Troop C clean up that mess. Can't say I'll miss that vending machine, though. I told you, Spitzer, that those things have no place in a scout camp. Full a' junk food and sugar water!"

Spitzer slapped his forehead. "Oh, let's not have that argument again, Walter! They are important sources of camp revenue." The two troop leaders went on bickering about vending machines and money, but I stopped listening. I wasn't buying Walter's raccoon theory either, so the mystery remained about who actually wrecked all that stuff. But all I cared about was that it wasn't me. I was off the hook.

For now.

FOOT FOR THOUGHT

As we helped Troop C clean up their wrecked cabin, I searched for that extra-large footprint, but with so many people walking everywhere, it must've gotten trampled. I wasn't sure what it meant, anyway. I hadn't met anyone in camp with feet that big!

After we cleaned up, I found a

few minutes alone to study my new handbook more closely. Honestly, I thought my smelly old handbook had better instructions in it than the new ones did. It was just cluttered with a few extra pictures, is all.

Okay a lot. Tons of crazy pictures and diagrams and, yes, monsters. Although the cover was all messed up, the title appeared before the book's

table of contents: *The Strange Scout's Handbook of Cryptozoology and Manners.*

Crypto-huh?

At the bottom of the title page it read, "Property of W. S., Strange Scout, First Class."

Strange Scout? I'd say. This W. S. person must've been the one who'd written all the notes. I mean, there were the normal chapters you'd expect in a scouting handbook, like "Tent Making Made Easy," but there were also crazy chapters like "Denetting a Sea Monster Without Getting Your Noggin Bitten Off" and "Categorizing Yeti Spoor in Polite Society."

The old handbook was a crazy mash-up of wilderness scouting tips and monster guide. According to the copyright, it had been published in 1908, which is like older than history itself, right? Maybe it was some kind of novelty book. Maybe it was W. S.'s idea of a joke.

But by that point I didn't care because that handbook had saved my behind.

That night was our first real campfire. Now a campfire may

sound cool at first, like roasting marshmallows and making s'mores and stuff, but for Troop D, it stunk. We waited for Walter at our cabin forever, but he never showed up. I figured he was probably napping somewhere and overslept. We finally went to the campfire without him, but

by then everyone else had eaten all of the marshmallows and chocolate. All we were left with were a few stale graham crackers. What were we supposed to do, roast those? You just try sticking a graham cracker on a stick.

Go on, try it. I'll wait.

"So," said Spitzer, as we gathered around the fire. "You scouts all know the legend of the Beastly Bigfoot of Bear Mountain, don't you?"

I rolled my eyes. Here came the spooky campfire stories. Grown-ups are so predictable.

"Tales of the creature date back to the Native American tribes," said Spitzer. "Tall as two men stacked one on top of the other. Lives way up the

mountain, and anyone who dares climb too high never comes back . . ."

Spitzer lowered his voice to a spooky whisper. "And on the night of the full moon, the beast howls as it hunts fresh prey! Kids, I'm told, are a particularly tasty delicacy!"

Suddenly, a shape appeared in the trees behind Spitzer!

"Hogwash!" it barked.

I gotta admit, it wasn't a very Bigfooty thing to say. That's because it wasn't a Bigfoot at all. It was a Walter. He was covered in thistles and his glasses were askew, but it was definitely him.

Ginger leaned over and whispered, "He's looking a little rough."

I elbowed Manuel to get his attention.

"Hmm?" said Manuel, looking up from his game. "Hey, I smell smoke."

"We're at a campfire, Manuel," I sighed.

"Oh, cool! Hope we get to make s'mores." Then he was back to his game. The kid was hopeless.

Meanwhile, the two troop leaders

were getting into a heated debate over the Bigfoot of Bear Mountain.

"I was just telling them a story, Walter," Spitzer was saying. "Relax. It was a lesson in folklore."

"It's a lesson in hogwash and hooper-nanny, and you should know better! Kids, Bigfoot is a shy creature, an omnivore who lives off berries and small varmints and avoids contact with people."

At that moment the clouds broke overhead and the moon finally appeared. It was round and yellow— a full moon!

Walter pointed up at it with his stick. "Now see there's the moon, nothing to be afraid of. Bigfeet don't eat kids and they certainly don't howl at the—"

"AARRROAROAAAARR!"

Something in the darkness let out a deep, growly howl. It sounded far off, just not far enough.

"AARRROAROAAAARR!"

We covered our ears, but the horrible sound grew louder. The trees shook, the mountain echoed until . . .

"BURRRRUP!"

And just like that it was over. We all looked at each other, but it was Ginger who finally said aloud what we all were thinking: "Wait a minute! Was that a burp?"

"Aw, c'mon, kids," said Spitzer, with a nervous laugh. "Probably just a bobcat. Or a moose."

Walter said nothing. He just adjusted his glasses and thoughtfully peered into the darkness.

Worriedly, I thought about that size-20 footprint I'd found outside Cabin C. And in case you were wondering, there have been exactly zero burping moose sightings on Bear Mountain, ever. I checked.

Toe-Tally Blown Away

That night I dreamed a shadowy figure peeked in our cabin window. I couldn't make out the face, but two big yellow eyes, like moons, stared back at me. I was frozen in place, with my sleeping bag pulled up almost over my head. It watched me for a long time, and when it finally stomped away, the ground shook.

Swimming was on the schedule for day two, so after breakfast we put on our suits. Normally I'd smear on enough sunscreen that I'd look like a shirtless mime, but Walter stopped me. "The swimming hole

is the only source of fresh drinking water for wildlife for miles," he said. "Chemicals might contaminate it. And there's plenty of shade this time of day. It's why we swim in the morning."

Spitzer and the other troops joined us, and together we marched through the woods. "You kids just wait until you see it," Walter was saying, as he led us on a small hike along a well-worn trail. "We've been teaching generations of Nature Scouts to swim here for I don't know how long. Even the scardiest ones learn to love the water by the time camp's over, ain't that right, Spitzer?"

Spitzer, for some strange reason, was blushing like a tomato.

Walter chuckled and kept on

talking. "We call it a swimming hole, but it's actually a limestone lake. The limestone keeps the acidity down, which otherwise can be a real problem with all the pollution nowadays. We keep our swim lessons strictly limited to one small area, so we don't disturb the thirsty critters that want to drink from the far side. If we're lucky, we might even be treated to a wildlife sighting—"

Walter's nature monologue was cut off by the sound of revving motors just up ahead. "What in tarnation?" he yelled, trying to be heard over the roar.

We rounded a bend and came to the shore. But instead of the peaceful lake Walter had described, what we found was more like . . . a carnival.

The placid lake had been turned into a Jet Ski raceway. A bunch of guys in uniforms that read "Weber's" were standing beneath a sign that read, "Watercraft Safety Brought to you by Weber's Jet Skis."

Walter's mouth fell open, and I'm pretty sure we all looked just as stunned. He turned to Spitzer. "What in tarnation is all this?"

"It's our corporate sponsorship," said Spitzer, defensively. "I keep telling you, we need revenue. And by partnering with Weber's Jet Skis, we're bringing this camp into the 21st century."

"Well, you can tell them to take all this junk back."

"Walter, be reasonable . . ."

"This here's a wildlife drinking hole," said Walter, "not just a swimming hole! How're they gonna drink with all these kerfangled machines churning up the mud and leaking motor oil all over the place? I thought you called yourself a Nature Scout!"

Spitzer started to get mad. "Tell you what, old man. Let the scouts decide: Kids, do you want nice, peaceful, boring old swimming lessons or do you want Jet Skis?"

He was immediately answered by a roar of "Jet Skis!" which quickly turned into a chant.

I hate to admit it, but I found myself chanting right along with them, even as Asma and Ginger shot me dirty looks. (Manuel was so into his game I don't think he even knew he was in his swim trunks.)

But come on! Jet Skis!

Butch shoved his way to the front, of course. "Yeah, who cares what that old fart says any—ouch!"

Ginger, who came up to Butch's waist, was standing on his foot and glaring up at the bully. "He may be an old fart, but he's our old fart!"

Believe it or not, Butch actually backed off. He grumbled something under his breath, but he didn't say another bad word about Walter that day.

I've heard it said that if you poke a bear, you're liable to lose a finger. Well, Ginger may be small, but if you poke her when she's mad (which is like

90 percent of the time), I suspect you'd
lose a finger, hand, arm, and maybe
even your head.

Anyway, Spitzer and Walter were
back to arguing and the rest of us . . .
I mean, come on! Jet Skis! Kids were
hooting and hollering as they skied
across the lake on 150 horsepower
of fun.

I was right about to join them. That is, until Asma and Ginger got in my way.

"Aw, come on!" I said. "Just one ride. Maybe Spitzer's right. Why do we owe Walter anything?"

Ginger exchanged a look with Asma

before answering. "Boy, you really don't get it yet, do you?"

"Get what? I get that we drew the short straw and got stuck with a grouchy old guy who'd rather tie knots than do anything fun."

Asma shook her head. "One, he defended you when Butch accused you of doing something you didn't do. And two, we didn't get Walter by chance. Think about it, Ben. We're Troop Dweeb. He volunteered to be our troop leader because . . . well, because nobody else wanted us."

Okay, I'll admit that at that moment I felt about 1 inch tall. Spitzer and Walter had stopped arguing, and it looked like Spitzer had won. Now Walter stood at the edge of the swimming hole, shoulders slumped, and all he could do was watch as the Jet Skis churned up the now-muddy water and a rainbow sheen of motor oil slowly spread across the lake.

Agony of De-Feet

alter was in a blue mood for the rest of the day, and shortly after dinner he disappeared back to his private cabin. I went to bed kind of blue myself. I couldn't shake the image of poor Walter standing at the edge of that swimming hole looking so defeated. And I couldn't shake the memory of what an ungrateful jerk I'd been.

The next morning I woke up to a bunch of yelling and carrying on. We stumbled, sleepily, out of our cabins to find junior troop leader Marcie trying in vain to calm down scouts who were running in every direction.

Bleary-eyed and groggy, I found Asma. "What's going on?"

"Walter is missing!" she said. "His cabin's a mess—just like what happened to Cabin C. And no one's seen Spitzer all morning."

Wow. You know that moment when you realize the grown-ups in charge are just people like you? That bad things can happen to them, too? I was having one of those moments as I pictured Walter's cabin all in shambles.

"There's the kid you should be talking to," shouted someone behind me. I turned and saw Butch pointing my way. Of course.

Junior troop leader Marcie was trying to calm him down, but the big bully was red-faced. "Hey, Billingsley, how'd you do it? How'd a little squirt like you manage to bust all those Jet Skis?"

Jet Skis?

"Someone trashed those, too," Asma explained. "It's nuts."

As Marcie led Butch away, Asma and I went to get a look at Walter's cabin. It was worse than I'd feared. Someone, or something, had nearly ripped the door off its hinges. Ginger and Manuel were standing a few yards away, near the trees. Ginger quickly waved us over.

She was holding a pair of thick black glasses with a single smashed lens. "These are Walter's! I found them here in the dirt. Without them, he's half-blind. What if he wandered off into the forest?"

"Walter could be hurt," I said. "For all we know he could be really close by, but no one's even searching for him."

Asma nodded. "Marcie's got her hands full here."

"I say we look for him," said Ginger. "Because if I stay here much longer, I'm going to punch Butch in his red face."

"We'll need to grab our hiking gear."

Asma started making a list: "Rations, canteens, first aid . . . "

Manuel, however, hesitated as he stared at his video game. "Uh, guys, I'm down to 3 percent power here. I need time to recharge the battery."

"We're talking about a human being who's gone missing!" said Asma.

"Technically, two," I said. I mean, Spitzer was human. Going by the textbook definition, anyway.

Ginger glared at Manuel. "Put down the game for a bit, jeez."

Manuel looked like we'd just suggested he flush his goldfish down a toilet. "Are . . . are you guys nuts? What if I lose my save point? There's no wireless out here!"

Manuel looked at us. He looked

toward the cabins. He looked back at us.

Ding! A red light started to blink on his video game. Manuel blanched and started sweating. His eyes darted this way and that, like a trapped animal's. (Seriously, he was superdramatic.)

"Fine!" shouted Manuel, and he stuffed his dying game into his

backpack. "But let's find that old dude and get back ASAP. This scouting thing is worse than Space Force Seven on nightmare mode."

GOING TOE TO TOE

It was one thing to talk about searching for Walter in those lonely mountain woods but another to actually do it. The four of us weren't exactly what you'd call master trackers. Fortunately, we didn't have to be because it wasn't long before we stumbled across a trail that was impossible to miss.

There were footprints in the soggy

forest floor. Big footprints, like the one I'd seen outside Troop C's cabin, only these led deeper into the forest.

"Whoa," said Manuel, placing his own foot inside one of the prints. "Some raccoons, huh?"

But no sooner had Manuel stepped into the footprint than we heard nearby cries for help.

We broke through the trees, expecting to find Walter hurt or in danger. Instead, we found Scoutmaster Spitzer trapped atop a lone tree perched on a cliff. On one side of the tree, the cliff ended in a steep drop. On the other was a giant, hairy beast.

He shook the tree as he roared. Bigfoot was real, all right. And boy did he look mad.

"BUURRUUP!" Bigfoot let out an enormous belch as he rubbed his stomach.

"See?" Ginger called to Spitzer. "That's no burping moose!"

"Uh, Ginger," I said. "I don't think Spitzer cares about that right now."

The tiny girl shrugged. "When I'm right, I'm right, is all."

"What do we do?" asked Manuel. "If Bigfoot keeps shaking that tree, Spitzer might fall over the cliff!"

He was right. We needed to act—fast. I reached into my backpack to see if I had some food or something we could lure Bigfoot away with, but I found the old handbook instead. I'd forgotten all about it!

"Eww!" said Asma, as she watched

me flip through the moldy pages. "What is that?"

"It's the scout handbook, the original one, I think. Look, I'll explain later." I was hoping the handbook had some useful advice on dealing with gassy monsters. I flipped to the chapter on Bigfoot and skimmed the page. Habitat . . . Avoidance (too late) . . . Care of . . .

"Here's something," I said. "An extremely agitated Bigfoot can be calmed down by the presence of others of its kind." I looked up. "Anyone see any more Bigfeet around here?"

"Nope," said everyone.

"Thought so. Okay, so . . . it says that in the absence of additional Bigfeet, a simple Bigfoot call will sometimes calm the creature . . . and it gives instructions on making the call right here. Looks complicated."

Manuel leaned over my shoulder. "Nah, it's just following directions, dude. Like cracking a new game! Lemme try."

He read over the page, mumbling to himself as he bent his fingers into a crazy knot. "Let's see, then you hold them up and blow like this . . ." Manuel blew into his fingers. "AAAUUURRAAAGGH!"

AAAAUUURRRAAAAGGHH!!

Whoa! It really sounded like a Bigfoot! Bigfoot must've thought so, too, because he stopped shaking the tree and listened.

"Do it again!" I whispered.

Manuel put his hands to his lips. "AAAAUUGGRRAGGH!"

This time he definitely got Bigfoot's attention.

"Uh, guys?" said Asma. "He's coming this way."

"What are we gonna do now?" asked Manuel.

HEAD OVER HEELS

h, let's not panic," I said, while frantically flipping the pages of the handbook. If we ran, we'd be abandoning Spitzer, plus I doubted we'd be able to outrun Bigfoot. If I couldn't find a better solution, we were all going to end up as toe jam. It was then that I spotted something scrawled in the margin next to "Bigfoot Calls."

The mysterious W. S. had written a bit of advice.

"Okay, I think we should try a . . . lullaby?"

"ARRROUUAGARRH!" Bigfoot roared. He was almost on top of us.

"I don't think 'Rock-a-Bye Baby' is going to help!" shouted Ginger.

"No, there are more instructions. Do as I do." I put my hands up to my mouth, just like Manuel had, only

instead of a loud call, I made a soft buzzing sound. Kind of like a hum. "Just a little air. Don't blow too hard."

Manuel, Asma, and Ginger did the same, and soon we'd created a little chorus of gentle humming. I have to admit—it even made me a little drowsy.

Slowly but surely, Bigfoot calmed down. The big creature plopped down on the uneven dirt, grabbed a large rock to use as a pillow, and drifted off to sleep.

I couldn't believe it. I mean, how many of you can say you've put a Bigfoot down for his nap?

Asma beamed. "Wow, we did . . . good. Didn't we?"

"No! You kids are going to get yourselves hurt!"

Spitzer had finally climbed down from his tree. He was still freaked out, but I guess I can't blame him. Bigfoot looked gentle enough now that he was snoozing, but a minute ago he was trying to shake the poor scoutmaster off a cliff.

"A-all right, scouts," Spitzer said, as he hurried over to us. "Time to head back to camp. It's not safe up here."

"But what about Walter," said Manuel.

"Yeah," said Ginger. "We weren't even looking for you. You're welcome, by the way."

Spitzer let out a frustrated sigh. "Right now Walter's not my responsibility, but you are . . ." His sentence drifted off as he got a good look at the handbook clutched in my fingers. "Billingsley! Where did you get that?"

"Uh, I found it."

Before I could stop him, Spitzer snatched the handbook away from me.

"Hey! Give that back!"

"You have no idea how dangerous this is, young man!"

"Says you! Without it, we'd be Bigfoot pancakes." I grabbed for my book, but Spitzer lifted it out of reach.

"Uh, guys?" said Manuel, but I ignored him. Spitzer was as bad a bully as Butch. Worse.

"Give it back! Give it back!"

RRRRRRRRRRRRRRR

"Uh, guys!"

"What?" Spitzer and I said at the same time. Asma and Ginger were slowly backing away as Manuel pointed to something directly behind me.

Slowly, Spitzer and I turned around. I was staring directly into a round, furry belly.

With all the shouting, we'd woken up Bigfoot.

12

No Small Feet

O-okay kids," said Spitzer. "Get behind me." The scoutmaster dropped the handbook and put himself between us and Bigfoot, even though his knees were literally shaking. Bigfoot, on the other hand, looked totally calm. No roaring. No stomping.

"Hey, look," said Asma. "He's not getting all growly this time."

"He's probably just deciding which of us to squish first," whispered Spitzer.

But then a bent, ragged shape stepped out of the trees. "Nah, I'm sure that if push came to shove, he'd definitely choose you, Spitzer."

It was Walter. Dirty, with burrs and

thorns stuck in his beard, he looked
like he had rolled around in a pile of
leaves. But he wasn't hurt.

The old scoutmaster squinted up
at Bigfoot. "Thing about Bigfoot is,
there's nothing a little nap won't cure.
You'll find that on page 334, Ben."

Me? Oh! I snatched the handbook
up off the ground and brushed it off.

Bigfoot let out a massive yawn and stretched. Then he broke out in a goofy grin.

Asma handed Walter his lost glasses. "Uh, we found these."

"There they are!" He put them on and squinted through the one good lens. "It'll have to do for now, I guess."

"Walter!" hissed Spitzer. "That creature tried to kill me!"

"Phooey," said Walter. "He was trying to save you, you nitwit. What were you thinking, climbing a tree like that? You coulda fallen to your death."

"But he was shaking the tree, we saw him—uh, no offense, Bigfoot," I added quickly.

But Walter shrugged. "I said he was trying to rescue Spitzer. I didn't say he was any good at it. Bigfeet aren't known for thinking more than one step ahead. Shaking him outta the tree probably seemed like a pretty good plan at the time. Didn't it, big guy?"

Bigfoot grunted.

"If Spitzer hadn't gone scrambling up that tree like a scared chicken when he saw Bigfoot in the first place—"

Spitzer threw up his hands. "Oh, here we go again. Blame me! I was trying to save you, you old kook."

Walter pointed a bony finger in Spitzer's face. "And who told you I needed saving?"

"Your cabin was a wreck! You're getting too old for this stuff, Walter."

"Well, if I don't do it, then who will?"

I glanced at Asma, Ginger, and

Manuel, but they looked just as bewildered as I felt. "Um, excuse me? But can one of you please tell us *what the heck is going on?!?*"

The two grown-ups went silent. Even Bigfoot looked a little taken aback. "Er, sorry," I said. "Didn't mean to raise my voice, but we have like a million questions."

"Like who wrecked the camp?" asked Asma.

"And what happened to you, Walter?" asked Ginger.

"And when do I get to play my game?" asked Manuel.

I held out the handbook. "Seriously. I found this book under the floor of our cabin. It's yours, isn't it? A guidebook for like some kind of . . . monster scouts?"

Our troop leader looked down at the book and smiled. "Well, don't ask me. It's not mine."

"Then who . . ."

Walter pointed his thumb at Spitzer, who looked absolutely depressed. "It's his!"

13

ONE FOOT FORWARD, TWO FEET BACK

ait a minute," I said to Walter. "This book has to be yours! The initials on the inside are W. S."

Walter nodded. "Which stands for

William Spitzer. Though he prefers Bill these days, don't you, William?"

Spitzer sighed. "I never wanted to see that thing again. I tried burying it under the floor of that horrible old cabin. I see now I should have burned it."

"But why? This book saved us!" I opened the book to the Bigfoot chapter. "So this is your handwriting, isn't it, Spitzer? You're the one who came up with the lullaby idea!"

"He's right, William," said Walter. "You always were good at caring for monsters."

But Spitzer turned his back on Walter and said nothing.

Ginger, her face getting redder by the second, asked, "Walter, what's going on?"

The old man scratched his beard. "I thought it would have been obvious by now. Why do you think I handpicked you to be in Troop D? It's not for everyone, you know. Cream of the crop only."

"Handpicked for Troop Dweeb?" I asked.

Walter waved his hand. "Pish-posh. You know, back when I was just a young scout, the D stood for something else—danger!"

"But what kind of handbook is that?" asked Asma. "Since when do Nature Scouts learn about monsters and stuff?"

"Since never," said Spitzer, sullenly. "That's not a Nature Scouts handbook, that's a Strange Scouts handbook."

"Strange Scouts?" I asked.

"See?" said Manuel. "We are dweebs."

But Walter shook his head. "No, no. Not that kind of strange. Strange as in rare, weird, and wonderful!"

Walter patted Bigfoot like you would a household pet. "Bigfeet don't get worked up over nothing. I recognized the signs right away— venturing too close to camp, all that howling business. I tried to calm him down myself, but when this fella gets worked up, he can be a handful. Got a bit roughed up in the process, lost my glasses, and got turned around in the dark."

He pulled a thistle burr out of his beard. "Ouch! Anyway, poor

William—eh, I mean Scoutmaster Spitzer—thought I was in trouble, and he came out here looking for me. He found Bigfoot instead, and well, I guess you can figure out the rest."

Spitzer snorted. Bigfoot let out another awful belch and immediately started whining.

"That's okay, big fella, it'll pass," said Walter. He patted Bigfoot on the arm. "See, it's the water in the swimming hole that done it. I told you that little lake was the only clean water for miles around, but all this Jet Ski nonsense . . . " He shot a look over at Spitzer, who turned a shade darker. "Poor Eugene only ventured into camp looking for clean water to drink."

Eugene? Still, I felt sorry for the

thirsty creature, so I took off my
canteen and handed it to Bigfoot, um,
I mean Eugene. "Here."

Eugene downed the contents of my
canteen in one gulp and let out a happy
sigh.

Walter nodded approvingly. "Well
done. But it's only a temporary fix.
C'mon, let's get back to camp. I promise
I'll make everything clear!"

14

TIME TO FOOT THE BILL

Eugene the Bigfoot smartly stayed hidden in the woods while we returned to Camp Nature. We told the others half the truth—that Walter had gotten lost in the night without his glasses, and Spitzer had set out to find him. Everyone was so relieved that they didn't ask too many questions. Then Walter and Spitzer set the whole camp on a new mission: earning our conservation badges by cleaning up the swimming hole. Over the next few days we hauled the wrecked Jet Skis away and skimmed the lake to get it clean.

We even got our very first wildlife sighting as a doe and her fawn crept down the shore to drink.

Well, I guess technically it was Troop D's second wildlife sighting. Can't get much wilder than Bigfoot, right?

Speaking of Bigfoot, Walter kept his word. After the cleanup, it was finally time for some real answers.

"The Strange Scouts were founded

at the same time as the Nature Scouts,"
Walter explained as Troop D gathered
back at the cabins. "Though the scouts
were kept classified because of their
unusual mission. Code name: Troop
Danger."

"What mission?" I asked.

The old scoutmaster gave me a wide
grin. "To be protectors of the weird!
You see, when President Theodore
Roosevelt founded the Nature Scouts,
he knew that the world's most precious

resource is nature—all nature, even the odd bits. There're all sorts of critters in this world, it's just that some are odder than others."

"You're talking about monsters," said Manuel.

"Exactly. The Sasquatch, the Chupacabra, the Yeti. Creatures like that got to remain kinda secret or else people will start to panic. And by and

The first Strange Scout badge
1905

large, all monsters want is to be left alone. That's where the Strange Scouts came in."

Walter slung a battered old duffel bag onto my bunk. "President Roosevelt came up with the idea of the Strange Scouts as a kind of goodwill organization. A way to educate certain young people about the handling and care of these creatures so that they could pass on what they'd learned and the monsters would continue to thrive. Because if we ruin the monsters' habitats, we're ruining our own planet."

Walter reached inside the duffel bag. "Unfortunately, our numbers kind of dwindled over the years, and I've had a hard time finding any young scouts who I felt were up to the challenge. William Spitzer was one of the last."

"Spitzer was a Strange Scout?" asked Asma.

"Yep. The best."

"Then why'd he quit?" I asked.

"That's a long story, but I'm afraid he lost his way somewhere back there. And now all this nonsense with the Jet Skis and vending machines . . . he forgot what scouting is really about.

Rest of his story ain't mine to tell.
Maybe he will someday."

Walter pulled out a small wooden
box. "Anyway, William Spitzer was the
last Strange Scout. Until now."

He flipped open the box lid and
revealed four shiny brass badges,
each one shaped like a really big
foot. "Polished these up special. Ben,
would you kindly turn to page 123
of your handbook and read aloud the

requirements for the Bigfoot Badge?"

Nervously (seriously, my hands were shaking), I flipped open the book. "Uh, it says, 'To be awarded the Bigfoot Badge, the junior scout must display acts of courage, kindness, and teamwork, as well as pass the challenge of using the Bigfoot Call on a genuine bigfoot specimen, preferably an irate one.'"

Walter pinned a shiny badge on my otherwise empty vest. "I'd say you all passed with flying colors. So I, Strange Scoutmaster Walter Simmons III, welcome you to the Strange Scouts and award you the prized Bigfoot Merit Badge."

Then he pinned badges on Manuel, Ginger, and Asma, too.

"Repeat after me," he said.

```
On my honor I will do my best:
To honor Mother Nature and all
  her creations, especially the
  monstrous ones,
To help my fellow citizens of the
  world,
To preserve oddity and strangeness
  in all its glory, especially my
  own,
Because uniqueness is never
  weakness.
```

We repeated the words.

Walter saluted us. "That's it! You're all Strange Scouts, Junior Class. Now turn to page 5 in the handbook and study the chapters on herding northeastern biting pukwudgies. That, and two-person rowing. This week was the easy part, scouts. From here on out, you've got your work cut out for you!"

HoW To HeLp BiGfOoT

(AND OTHER FOREST FRIENDS)

Bigfeet dwell primarily in the deciduous forest biome, where temperate forests of trees lose their leaves with the changing seasons. You might think that these forests are common, but genuine deciduous forests become rarer each year. How can we help? One way is to visit a national park today! Spending time in the beauty and wonder of our protected parklands is the first step to becoming a Strange Scout! Learn more by visiting the National Parks Service at nps.gov/kids.

MATTHEW CODY is  the acclaimed children's author of several popular books, including the award-winning Supers of Noble's Green trilogy: *Powerless*, *Super*, and *Villainous*. He lives in New York City with his wife and son.

STEVE LAMBE is an  Emmy Award-winning animator for TV shows such as *The Fairly OddParents*, *Teen Titans Go!*, and *The Mighty B!* He has also illustrated several books in the Golden Book series. He lives in Ontario, Canada, with his wife and son.

Coming Soon